GREAT CAT

GREAT CAT

by David McPhail

A Unicorn Book   E. P. Dutton   New York

Library of Congress Cataloging in Publication Data

McPhail, David M.   Great Cat
A Unicorn book.

Summary: Because of her size, Great Cat, the biggest
cat that ever lived, causes the neighbors to fear for
their children's safety. Therefore, Great Cat and Toby
move to an island where they rescue a sinking boatload
of children.
[1. Cats—Fiction]   I. Title
PZ7.M2427Gs 1982   [Fic]   81-12654
ISBN 0-525-45102-1   AACR2

Published in the United States by E. P. Dutton, Inc.,
2 Park Avenue, New York, N.Y. 10016

Published simultaneously in Canada by Clarke,
Irwin & Company Limited, Toronto and Vancouver

Editor: Emile McLeod   Designer: Claire Counihan

Printed in Hong Kong by South China Printing Co.
First Edition   10 9 8 7 6 5 4 3 2 1

for Sandra and Jaime
who suffered long and patiently
the birth of Great Cat

and
to Bob and Barney
who were so good
to us,
always,

Great Cat was the biggest cat that ever lived.

No one knew where Great Cat came from, or how she got to be so big. She just appeared one night on Toby's doorstep. She was only a kitten then, but she was as big as a full-grown lion.

Toby had always wanted a kitten, so he invited Great Cat into his kitchen, where he gave her a bowl of milk. Then another bowl, and another. And that was the start of a wonderful friendship.

As she grew, Great Cat needed more and more food. Every day she drank gallons of milk and ate dozens of fish.

Toby bought a cow so Great Cat would have enough milk.

He bought a boat, and every morning before going to work, Toby went fishing.

The bigger Great Cat grew, the more fish she ate and the more fish Toby had to catch.

One day Toby was so tired from catching all those fish that he fell asleep at his job and was fired.

Toby enjoyed being home all day with Great Cat. They went for walks, and Great Cat let the neighborhood children ride on her back.

But the mothers and fathers were afraid for their children.

"Great Cat must go!" they told Toby. "She is so big, she might hurt someone!"

"If Great Cat goes, *I* go too!" said Toby.

So he sold his house, and moved with Great Cat and the cow to a small island in the ocean.

They missed the children. But there was plenty
of green grass for the cow, and the ocean was
full of fish for Toby and Great Cat.

They built a small house out of driftwood and
straw.

Toby and Great Cat fished and explored the island.

After supper, Toby read to Great Cat until it was time for bed.

One morning there was a terrible storm. Great Cat and Toby were watching the waves when they heard cries for help. They saw a small boat tossing wildly.

Toby started to drag his own boat to the water,
but Great Cat jumped into a crashing wave.

Great Cat swam until she reached the sinking
boat.

Someone in the boat threw a rope to Great Cat.
She grabbed it. Holding the rope between her teeth,
Great Cat swam back toward shore, pulling the boat.

Great Cat struggled through the waves.
When she got close to shore, Toby helped her pull
the boat up onto the beach.

Then Toby saw that the boat was filled with
children, who jumped out of the boat and hugged
Great Cat and Toby.

Toby built a fire and warmed some milk for
Great Cat and the children.

Slowly the storm passed, and the sea grew calm enough for the children to return to their camp on a nearby island.

As the children sailed away, Toby called after them, "Come back and see us!"

And they did, often.

David McPhail is the tallest illustrator of children's books who ever lived in Tamworth, New Hampshire.

He is a young man, but as big as a full-grown giant.

The title display type and the initial capital letter of the text are Goudy Bold. All other type is Galliard Bold. The full-color art was painted with watercolors.

The book was printed and bound by South China Printing Co., Hong Kong.